and the Silent Night

Roger Har

Original concept by
Roger Hargreaves

Written and illustrated by
Adam Hargreaves

EGMONT

Mr Quiet is a sensitive fellow.

Loud noises make him very nervous.

Unfortunately, for Mr Quiet, he lives in a place called Loudland.

Which is exactly that.

LOUD!

And at Christmas time, Loudland is an especially loud place.

Which means that Mr Quiet, unlike you and I, does not look forward to Christmas.

Poor Mr Quiet.

At Christmas time there are all the Christmas card deliveries, delivered by the Loudland postman, Mr Stamp.

Who is not called Mr Stamp because of the stamps you put on envelopes, but because he stamps his feet as he delivers the post.

STAMP! STAMP! STAMP! Up Mr Quiet's path.

SLAM! Would go the letterbox.

And then STAMP! STAMP! STAMP! Back down the path.

Every morning.

For weeks!

There were all the jolly Loudland people greeting each other on the street.

"HAPPY CHRISTMAS!"

"AND A HAPPY CHRISTMAS TO YOU!"

"AND A HAPPY NEW YEAR!"

They were so loud that it was like being at a football match.

And there were the carol singers.

In Loudland the carol singers do not just sing.

They bellow!

At the very top of their voices.

Poor Mr Quiet would turn out the lights and hide behind his sofa and pretend he was not at home.

But he could still hear them.

And to make matters even worse, every year,
Mr Noisy would come to stay.

Mr Noisy lives in a place where they do not like noise
so he likes to go to Loudland for his Christmas holiday
where he can be as loud as he likes. Which, as you
can imagine, is very loud indeed!

On Christmas morning, Mr Noisy would turn on the radio at full volume and sing along to the Christmas carols.

It was so loud it made the tea cups rattle in their saucers!

You could have heard Mr Noisy in another country!

Then there was Christmas lunch.

And crackers!

Loudland crackers.

BANG!

BANG!

Like a cannon being fired.

And of course, Mr Noisy eats with his mouth open.

CHOMP! CHOMP! CHOMP!

Through the turkey.

CHOMP! CHOMP! CHOMP!

Through the Christmas pudding.

What a racket.

Mr Noisy could not even open his presents quietly.

CRACKLE! CRACKLE! CRACKLE!

Went the paper each time he unwrapped one.

Poor Mr Quiet.

But that was last Christmas.

This Christmas something different happened.

Something magical.

It snowed!

Now, everyone likes snow, but this year it snowed and snowed and snowed until all the roads were deep with snow, right to the top of the hedges.

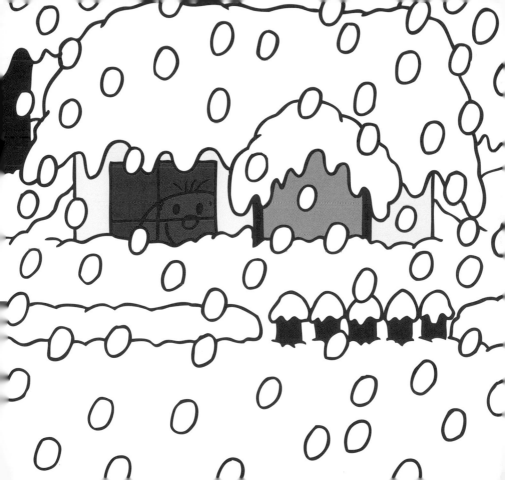

Which caused chaos.

But not for Mr Quiet.

Things went really rather well for Mr Quiet.

There was no loud Mr Stamp.

He was stuck at the post office.

There were no loud jolly people on the streets.

They were all stuck at home.

And there were no loud carol singers.

They got stuck in the snow.

But the very best thing of all was a phone call from Mr Noisy saying that he wouldn't be able to come to visit.

So this year, Mr Quiet had a very quiet Christmas.

No loud radio.

No loud crackers.

No loud chomping at dinner.

And no loud crackling wrapping paper.

The only thing that Mr Quiet could hear, very faintly, was the sound of carol singing.

Very quiet carol singing.

Just the sort of carol singing that Mr Quiet likes.

Who was it?

Why, it was Mr Noisy.

I told you, you could hear him from another country!

And what was Mr Noisy singing?

Have a guess...

That's right!

Silent Night!